Dear Parents:

Congratulations! Your child is taking the first steps on an exciting journey. The destination? Independent reading!

STEP INTO READING® will help your child get there. The program offers five steps to reading success. Each step includes fun stories and colorful art or photographs. In addition to original fiction and books with favorite characters, there are Step into Reading Non-Fiction Readers, Phonics Readers and Boxed Sets, Sticker Readers, and Comic Readers—a complete literacy program with something to interest every child.

Learning to Read, Step by Step!

Ready to Read Preschool–Kindergarten
• big type and easy words • rhyme and rhythm • picture clues
For children who know the alphabet and are eager to begin reading.

Reading with Help Preschool–Grade 1
• basic vocabulary • short sentences • simple stories
For children who recognize familiar words and sound out new words with help.

Reading on Your Own Grades 1–3
• engaging characters • easy-to-follow plots • popular topics
For children who are ready to read on their own.

Reading Paragraphs Grades 2–3
• challenging vocabulary • short paragraphs • exciting stories
For newly independent readers who read simple sentences with confidence.

Ready for Chapters Grades 2–4
• chapters • longer paragraphs • full-color art
For children who want to take the plunge into chapter books but still like colorful pictures.

STEP INTO READING® is designed to give every child a successful reading experience. The grade levels are only guides; children will progress through the steps at their own speed, developing confidence in their reading. The F&P Text Level on the back cover serves as another tool to help you choose the right book for your child.

Remember, a lifetime love of reading starts with a single step!

For my mother, Gerry Mitchell—
with love and appreciation
—M.M.

For Manase, my forever favorite
wizard. Your magic comes from
your big heart! Love you.
—S.C.

Visit us on the Web!
StepIntoReading.com
rhcbooks.com

Educators and librarians, for a variety of teaching tools, visit us at RHTeachersLibrarians.com

Library of Congress Cataloging-in-Publication Data
Names: Meadows, Michelle, author. | Cloud, Sawyer, illustrator.
Title: Maxie Wiz and her dragon / by Michelle Meadows; illustrations by Sawyer Cloud.
Description: First edition. | New York: Random House Children's Books, [2023] |
Series: Step into reading. Step 1 | Audience: Ages 4–6. | Audience: Grades K–1. |
Summary: When her dragon gets too big for the castle, a little wizard uses magic to fix the problem.
Identifiers: LCCN 2022004678 | ISBN 978-0-593-57027-2 (trade paperback) |
ISBN 978-0-593-57028-9 (library binding) | ISBN 978-0-593-57029-6 (ebook)
Subjects: CYAC: Stories in rhyme. | Magic—Fiction. | Dragons—Fiction. |
LCGFT: Stories in rhyme. | Picture books.
Classification: LCC PZ8.3.M4625 Max 2023 | DDC [E]—dc23

Printed in the United States of America
10 9 8 7 6 5 4 3 2 1
First Edition

This book has been officially leveled by using the F&P Text Level Gradient™ Leveling System.

Maxie Wiz
and her
Dragon

by Michelle Meadows

illustrated by Sawyer Cloud

Random House New York

Maxie Wiz

casts a spell.

Baby dragon
in its shell!

Hocus-pocus!

Time to hatch!

Hello, Dragon!

Perfect match!

Dragon, Dragon
loves to play.

Swimming in the
swamp all day.

Hocus-pocus!
No more slime.

Clean and shiny.
Goodbye, grime!

Dragon, Dragon
wants to eat.

Looking for a
tasty treat.

Hocus-pocus!

Make a snack.

Magic cupcakes
in a stack.

Dragon, Dragon,
tall and wide.

Grows too big
to fit inside.

Hocus-pocus!

Stretch this place.

Now our castle
has more space.

Dragon, Dragon,
kiss good night.

Tossing, turning,
squeeze in tight.

Hocus-pocus!
Bigger bed.

Make more room
for us to spread.

Dragon, Dragon
blinks and stares.

Hocus-pocus!
Teddy bears.

Huggle, snuggle.

Not one peep.

Good night, Dragon.
Time to sleep.